Sophie Corrigan

PUGTATO

finds a thing

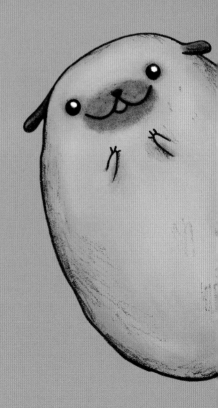

ZONDER**kidz**

This is Pugtato.
He's a simple, good spud.

He can often be found
digging in the mud.

One day as he planted some seeds in the ground,
he dug up a Thing all shiny and round.

Pugtato thought hard,
but he hadn't a clue
what this Thing was
or what it could do.

So he cleaned up the Thing
and took it away
to show his best spuddies
to see what they'd say.

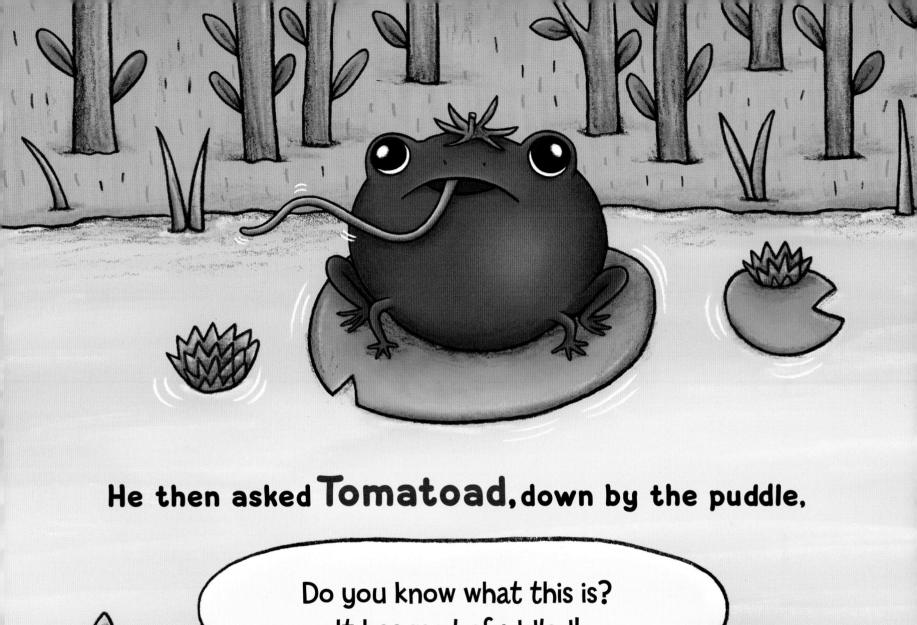

He then asked **Tomatoad**, down by the puddle,

Do you know what this is?
It has me befuddled!

"That Thing is for bouncing,"
he croaked.
"What a treasure!"

And he gave it a wet,
bouncy lick for good measure.

"Oh, this won't do!" Pugtato said with a sigh.
And he took Thing away to give Purrsnip a try.

Purrsnip was napping, which was not a surprise,
but a woof from his friend made him open his eyes.

Sorry to wake you,
but I am confused!
Can you tell me how this little
Thing should be used?

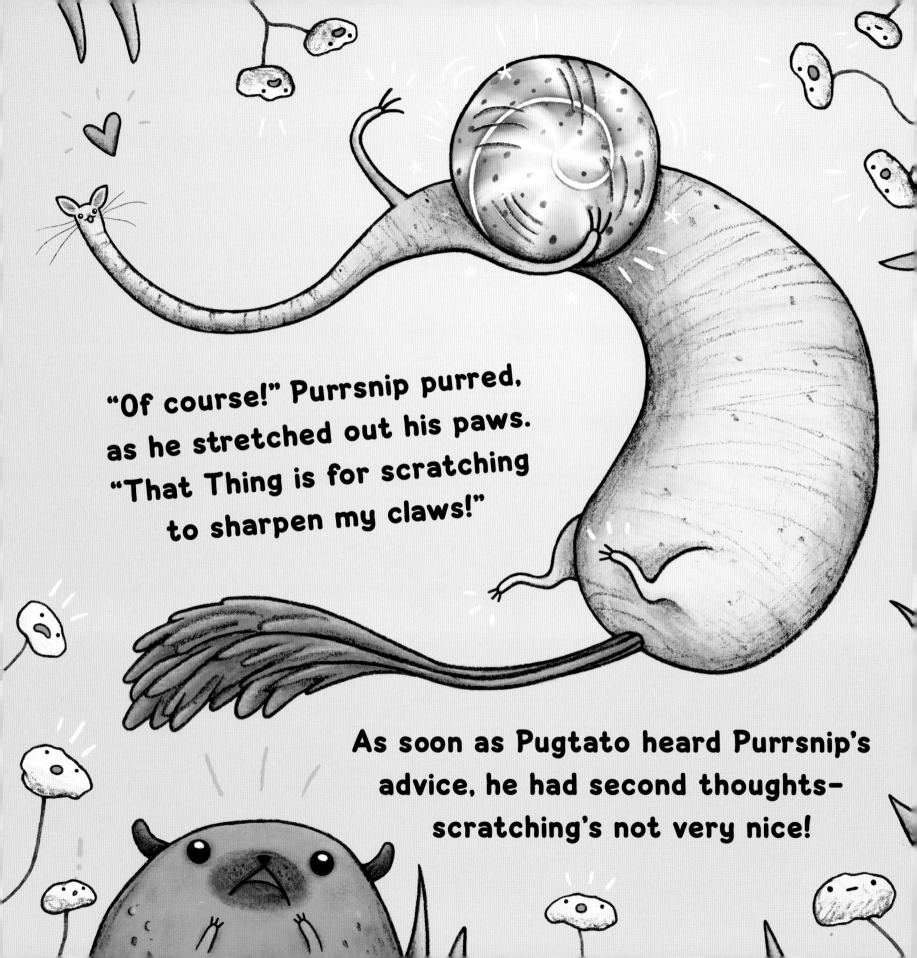

"Of course!" Purrsnip purred, as he stretched out his paws. "That Thing is for scratching to sharpen my claws!"

As soon as Pugtato heard Purrsnip's advice, he had second thoughts—scratching's not very nice!

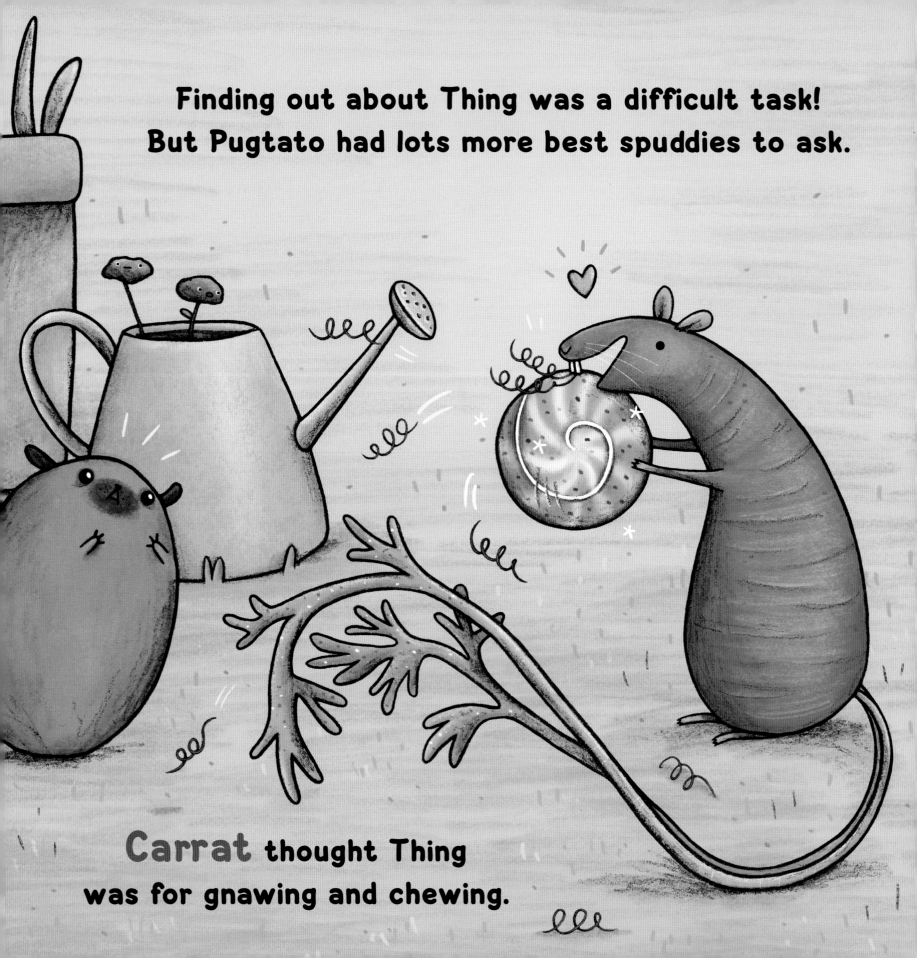

Finding out about Thing was a difficult task!
But Pugtato had lots more best spuddies to ask.

Carrat thought Thing
was for gnawing and chewing.

And **Cowbbage**, well,
she simply stared at it, MOOOO-ing.

Pugtato showed Thing to the three
Brussels Snouts.

They snuffled and snorted
that Thing all about.

Right to **Collieflower**,
who gave chase to the Thing!

Collieflower was sure
a new toy had been found,
as he barked at Thing loudly
and tossed it around!

When he came to the field, there, mysterious and tall,
stood Unicorn on the Cob, the wisest of all.

Hello! Do you know what this
strange Thing might be?
Like everyone else, you're much
smarter than me!

"Oh, little Pugtato,
you must follow your heart.
For it holds all the answers
and sets you apart."

Pugtato stared hard at the Thing he had found.

Perhaps it's just shy, so it hides underground?

I may not know much
but I know when I see ...
a Thing that needs hugs,

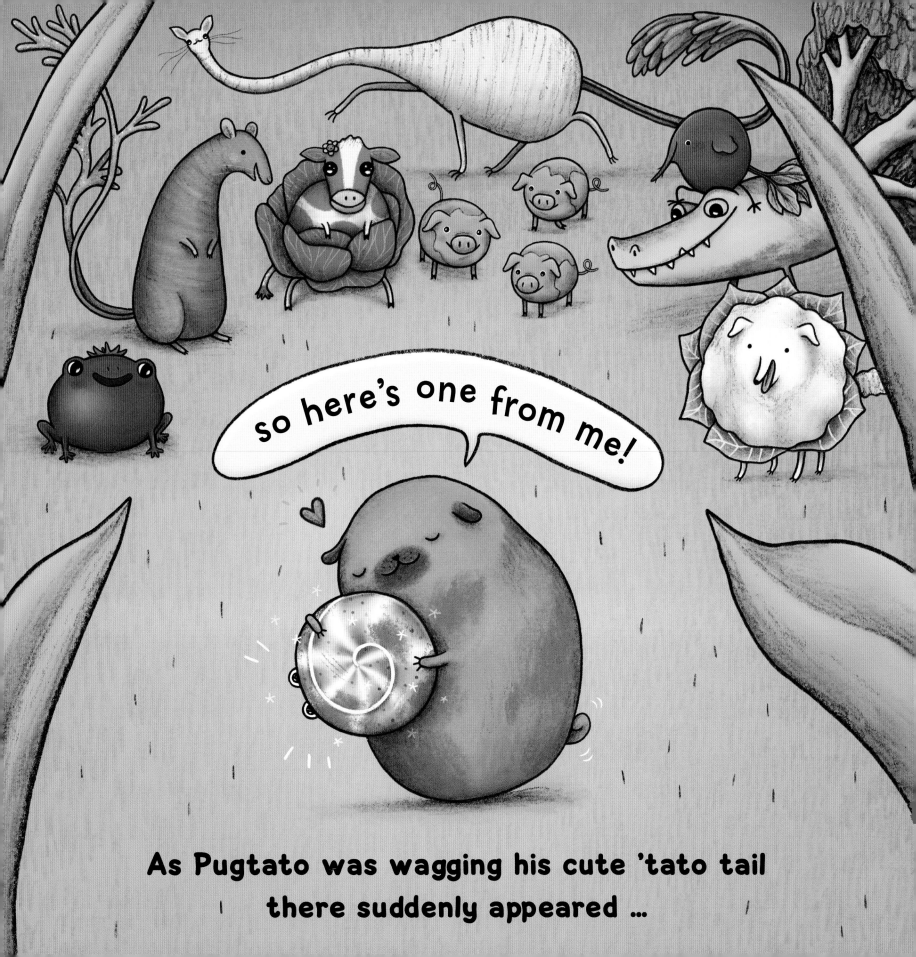

As Pugtato was wagging his cute 'tato tail
there suddenly appeared ...

a Curly Kale Snail!

Pugtato was happy (despite being muddy).
"I know what you are,
you're my newest, best spuddy!"

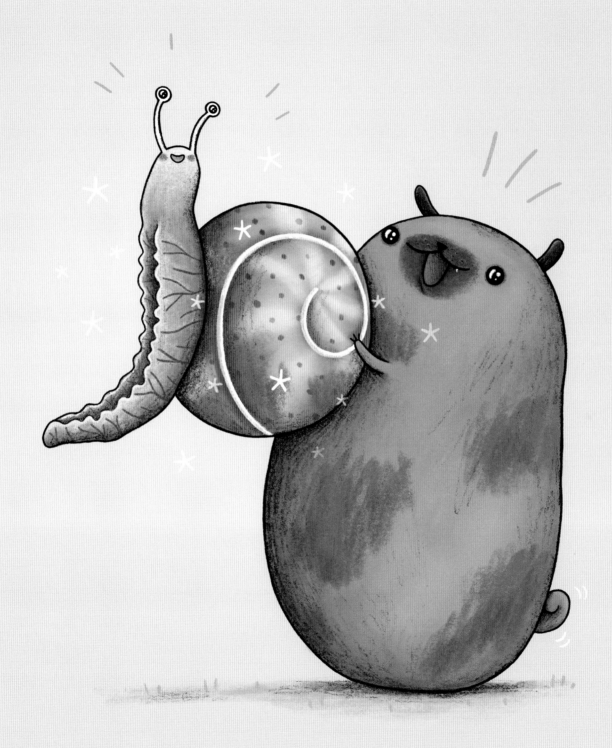

This is Pugtato. He may not feel smart.
But he's wiser than most when he follows his heart.

For my Nan,
who loved a good spud.
–S. C.

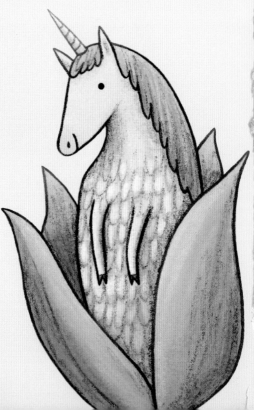

ZONDERKIDZ

Pugtato Finds A Thing
Copyright © 2020 by Sophie Corrigan
Illustrations © 2020 by Sophie Corrigan

Requests for information
should be addressed to:

*Zonderkidz, 3900 Sparks Dr. SE,
Grand Rapids, Michigan 49546*

Hardcover ISBN 978-0-310-76781-7

Ebook ISBN 978-0-310-76786-2

Editor: Barbara Herndon
Design: Cindy Davis

Printed in China

20 21 22 23 24 25 /DSC/ 13 12 11 10 9 8 7 6 5 4 3 2 1